Contents

A Hot Dog Day   7

Farmer Donald's Pumpkin Patch 63

Look Before You Leap 87

Minnie's Rainbow 111

Up, Up And Away 135

A Hot-Dog Day

Things for Picnic:
Tablecloth
Napkins
Plates
Fruit Salad
Lemonade
Corn on the Cob
Hot Dogs
Buns
Ketchup
Mustard

By Sheila Sweeny Higginson
Illustrated by the Disney Storybook Artists

Minnie woke up early. She opened the window to let in the cool morning air. Outside, the birds were chirping. The sun peeked through the trees on the horizon.

"What a lovely day!" Minnie said. "It's the perfect day for a picnic. The first thing I need to do is make invitations."

Things for Picnic:
Tablecloth
Napkins
Plates
Fruit Salad
Lemonade
Corn on the Cob
Hot Dogs
Buns
Ketchup
Mustard

Minnie looked over the invitations she had made. "My friends will be so happy to receive these pretty cards," she said. Then she sat down and wrote a list of all the things she would need for the picnic – a tablecloth, plates, napkins and food, of course! When she was finished, she headed out the door.

But before she had gone very far, she turned around.
"Silly me," she said. "I forgot to bring something to hold all my picnic goodies.
And I really should bring along my new tablecloth, and napkins and some plates.
Then I won't have to come back for them later."

Minnie looked around the Clubhouse for something that was big enough for all the picnic supplies. She soon found her basket on a high shelf.

"That will be perfect for my picnic," she said.

"But how will I reach it?" Minnie asked. "Should I use a fishhook and try to reel it in? Or could I lasso it with that rope?" she wondered aloud, looking at the rope that was hanging on the wall. Seeing her pogo stick, she thought about jumping high to grab the basket.

"Mmm," she finally said, "maybe using this stepladder would be the best choice."

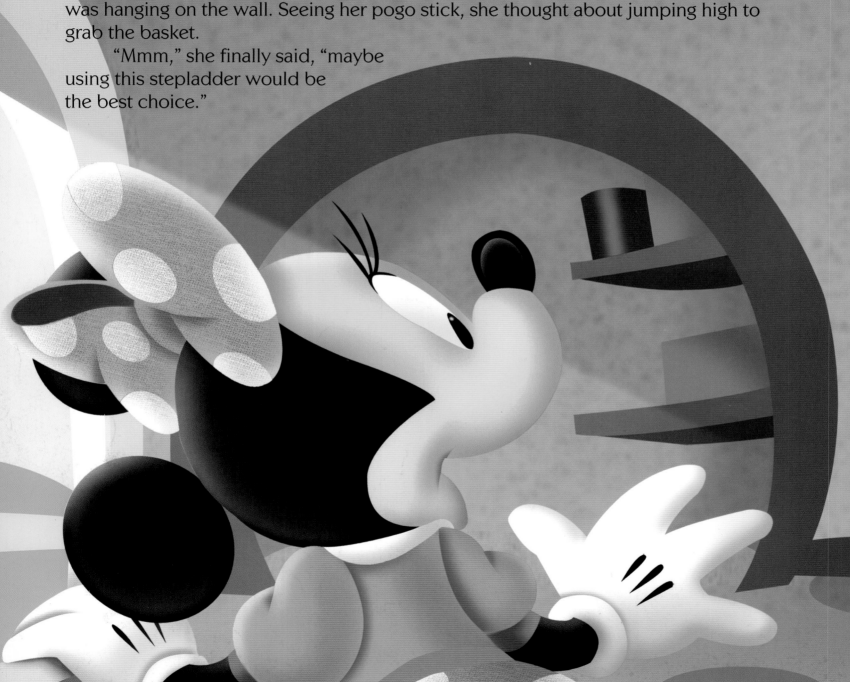

A moment later, Daisy strolled by. There on the lawn, she saw Minnie's picnic basket.

"What's this?" she wondered aloud. "Minnie is planning a picnic? I love picnics!"

Daisy read Minnie's shopping list and decided to make a fruit salad to share with all the guests. She picked up the basket and headed toward the blueberry bushes at the end of the road.

Before long, Daisy had picked many, many blueberries. She filled her handbag with them. She tasted a few, just to make sure they were sweet enough for her friends.

16

"Oh, my," she said to herself when she could hold no more berries. "I need to get a bowl – one that's big enough to hold all the fruit for the salad."

So off she went, forgetting the basket under a bush.

Minnie returned to the garden. She saw that her picnic basket was missing!
"My picnic basket!" she cried. "Where could it be?"
Minnie looked behind the daffodils. She looked under the tulips. She retraced her steps back to the Clubhouse. But she could not find it.

"Oh, no!" Minnie said, sighing. "My picnic is over, and it never even started!" Sadly, she plopped into a chair.
Even the flowers looked glum.

Back in the kitchen, Daisy found a small bowl, but the bowl was not large enough to hold the berries. So she poured them into a medium-size bowl. That, too, soon overflowed. Finally, Daisy put all the blueberries into a large bowl.

"Perfect!" she said. "There's even room left over for me to add some watermelon."

Daisy headed out the door, thinking about the delicious fruit salad she would soon make for her friends.

Daisy went to the watermelon patch behind the Clubhouse. There were six juicy watermelons growing on the vine. She looked at them all and decided not to take the biggest one.

"That one would be too heavy for me to lift," she said to herself.

She decided not to take the smallest one. "That one would not have enough juicy fruit inside."

She didn't pick any of the yellow ones, either, because yellow melons need more time to grow.

She wondered aloud, "Which one is just right?"

Daisy did not choose the biggest or the smallest or any of the yellow melons. That left just one – the medium-sized green melon. Daisy cut it open and was very happy to see juicy red fruit inside.

"This melon smells so sweet!" she declared as she carefully cut the fruit into cubes.

As Daisy mixed her salad, Donald was taking a walk down the road near the blueberry bush. He spotted a basket and looked inside.

"Well, finally!" Donald exclaimed. "Someone is planning a picnic! And best of all, there will be lemonade at the picnic. I love lemonade." Donald decided that he would make the lemonade himself.

Taking the basket with him, Donald headed off into town to buy the ingredients for his lemonade.

Things for Picnic:
Tablecloth
Napkins
Plates
Fruit Salad
Lemonade
Corn on the Cob
Hot Dogs
Buns
Ketchup

23

Daisy finished mixing the blueberries and the watermelon in the bowl.
"All that this salad needs to be perfect," she announced, "is something yellow."
She remembered that there was a pineapple in the kitchen.

Before getting the pineapple, Daisy looked around for Minnie's basket.
"Oh, no! Where could it be?" she cried. She tried to remember where she had seen it last.
"The blueberry bush!" she shouted as she ran down the road.

Daisy looked under the blueberry bush. She looked next to the blueberry bush. She even looked behind the blueberry bush. But she could not find Minnie's basket.

"I guess I should just make a fruit salad for everyone," Daisy said to herself.

Donald couldn't wait to make his special lemonade. He arrived at the grocery store carrying the basket and the list.

"Well, let me see," he said. "I'll buy some sugar and a jar of red cherries. And I'll need six lemons – and my secret ingredient: one lime."

Things for Picnic:
Tablecloth
Napkins
Plates
Fruit Sal
Lemon

Donald looked at the lemons. He thought they all looked delicious. But one seemed especially plump and juicy. Donald reached for the biggest lemon.

"Not that one!" the shopkeeper shouted to Donald. "Don't take one from the bottom because—"

But it was too late. The lemons fell down on Donald and tumbled onto the floor. Donald quickly ran out the door after buying his lemons, and left Minnie's basket behind.

Donald headed back to the Clubhouse.

"My goodness!" he quacked, looking in the windows. "Minnie and Daisy sure do look grumpy. Well, they'll feel better when I serve them my super-duper, secret-recipe lemonade."

Donald cut each lemon – and one lime – in half. He squeezed each half in the juicer. Next, he slid a straw through each cherry and mixed some cherry juice in with the lemon and lime juice. Then he measured out the right amount of sugar, poured water into the pitcher, added the juice and some ice, and stirred.

"This is guaranteed to perk up my grumpy friends!"

On this sunny morning, Goofy was in town, taking his kitten, Mr Pettibone, for a walk. When Mr Pettibone spotted a lemon rolling down the sidewalk, he pounced on it.

Goofy looked inside the store and saw the shopkeeper picking up all the rolling lemons. He began to help. Just as he was about to pick up the last lemon, something caught his eye.

It was Minnie's basket with a letter addressed to him.

"Oh, boy!" Goofy said when he read the invitation. "There's nothing I like more than a picnic!"

He looked at the shopping list. "Seems to me that someone needs to make some corn on the cob. There's nothing I like more than corn on the cob – except picnics!" he said. So, off he went towards the cornfield, taking the basket with him.

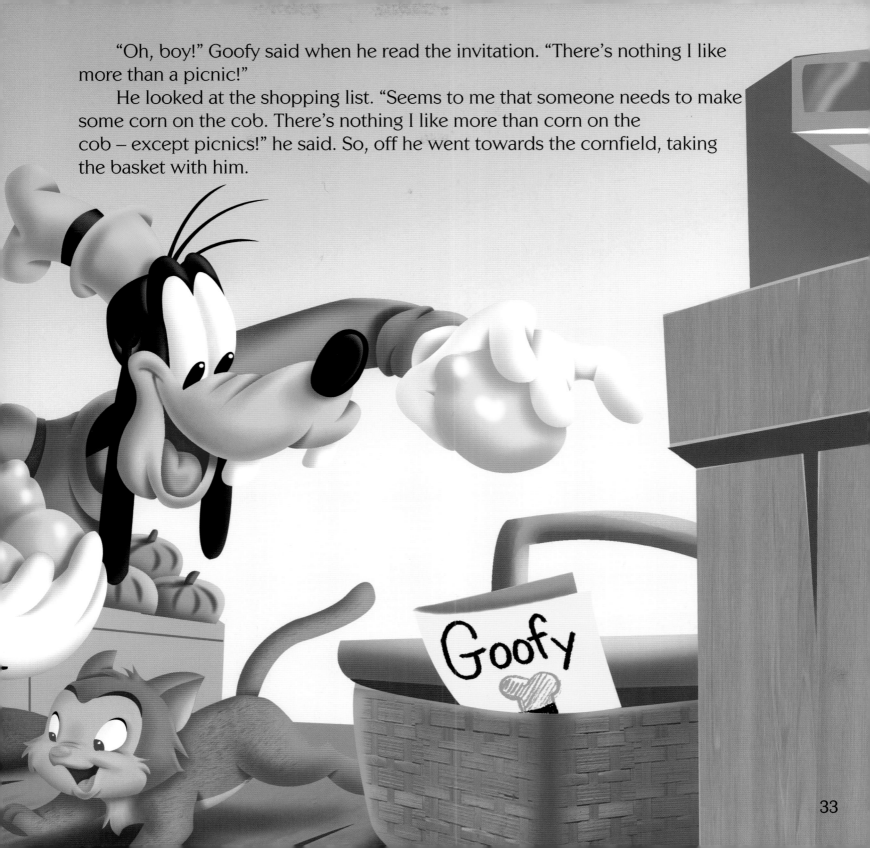

Goofy

33

Goofy walked quickly down the road towards the cornfield. The corn had grown high under the warm sun. It was even taller than he was! As he approached the rows of stalks, Goofy could almost taste the corn.

"Look at those big ears!" he exclaimed, wetting his lips.

Things for Picnic:
~~Tablecloth~~
~~Napkins~~
~~Plates~~
~~Fruit Salad~~
~~Lemonade~~
~~Corn on the Cob~~
Hot Dogs

"How many cobs do we need?" Goofy wondered aloud. "Well, Pluto doesn't eat corn, so I don't need to count him. Minnie will want one. Daisy will want one. That's two, so far. Donald will probably have two. So, two plus two equals four. Mickey will want one. That's five. And I'll have five. So all together, I need to pick ten ears of corn."

Goofy was so excited about getting back to the Clubhouse to cook the corn, that he left the basket behind! He was so happy that he sang a corny little song as he walked:

Corn, corn, wonderful corn.
I could eat it night and morn!
Cornflakes, corn bread, corn dogs, too.
Corn on the cob for me and you!

Goofy looked in the kitchen for the largest pot he could find. He filled it with water and waited until the water boiled.

Meanwhile, Donald had gone into the garden to pick a few mint leaves to add to the lemonade. He thought it would be a good idea to put the pitcher into Minnie's basket. He looked around.

"Uh, oh," he said. "Where's the basket? Could I have left it at the store?"

Donald ran back to town. At the store, he looked under the counter. He looked behind the new stack of lemons.

"This is terrible!" he whispered to himself when he realized that the picnic basket was gone. Then he tiptoed outside and headed back to the Clubhouse.

Meanwhile, Mickey and Pluto were out for a drive. There was only one thing Pluto liked more than riding in Mickey's car, and that was running through the cornfield. So Mickey stopped the car to give Pluto a chance to run around.

"What's this?" Mickey said when he saw the basket. He recognized it right away. "This is Minnie's basket," he said, picking it up. Then he saw the invitations inside. "Hey, Pluto!" he called. "Minnie is having a picnic, and we're invited! Let's get these last things on her list before heading back to the Clubhouse."

41

Back at the Clubhouse kitchen, Goofy placed the corn in hot water, along with a pinch of sugar and a dash of salt.

"I think I'll put this plate of corn into Minnie's basket now," Goofy said. That's when he realized that he'd left the basket back at the cornfield.

Goofy ran out of the door, straight towards the cornfield. He looked high. He looked low. Then he looked very, very sad.

"Gawrsh!" he said, "I feel just awful about losing Minnie's basket." Slowly, he walked back towards the Clubhouse with his long ears hanging down.

At the store, Mickey piled the hot dogs, buns, ketchup and mustard onto the counter.

"Well, that's about it, Pluto," he said. Then he glanced at the clock.

Corn on the Cob
Hot Dogs
uns
up

"Golly! It's almost noon. We'd better hurry back to the Clubhouse for Minnie's picnic."
Out of the door they went.

It was almost lunchtime, but Minnie wasn't hungry.
"The next time I plan a picnic," she said to herself, "I'll make sure that I don't lose the invitations and the picnic basket!" She decided to take a walk. "Maybe I can pretend I'm having a picnic with my friends," she said. She took along her flowers.

At almost the same moment, Daisy decided to take her bowl of fruit salad to the picnic table.

"Maybe some of my friends will be at the playground and would like to share this salad," she sighed.

47

Donald remembered that the picnic was planned for noon at the playground, so he grabbed his pitcher and headed out.
"All you really need for a picnic is my special lemonade," Donald said to himself.

Goofy, too, decided to bring his plate of corn to the playground. "Golly, I sure hope the picnic is still on," he said as he walked towards the picnic area. Then he smiled and said, "Otherwise, I guess I'll have to eat all this corn myself."

"Looks like we're just in time, old buddy," Mickey said to Pluto as they neared the playground.

"I hope we're not too late, Minnie," Mickey said as he walked towards his friends.

Minnie was speechless while her friends set the table.
Finally, she said, "I lost my basket and all the invitations in the garden
this morning. So I thought my picnic was ruined."

"I'm sorry," Daisy said. "I found your basket in the garden and decided to make a fruit salad."

54

"But then I lost it by
the blueberry bush."

55

"Well, actually, I found your basket by the blueberry bush," Donald said. "And I decided to make lemonade. But then I lost the basket at the grocery store."

"I found it at the grocery store," Goofy said. "And I decided to make corn on the cob. But then I left your basket in the cornfield."

"Pluto and I found your basket in the cornfield," Mickey said, "and we decided to get the hot dogs, buns and fixings."

Then he turned to Minnie and said, "I hope you're not angry with us, Minnie."

"How could I be angry?" Minnie said as she looked at all of her friends and the tasty foods they had made for her picnic. "You're the best friends in the whole world."

Everyone enjoyed Daisy's fruit salad, Donald's lemonade, Goofy's corn on the cob and the wonderful hot dogs and buns that Mickey prepared.

"This is the best picnic ever!" Minnie declared.

"Hot dog!" Mickey agreed.

The End

Farmer Donald's Pumpkin Patch

By Susan Ring
Illustrated by Loter, Inc.

"Look at this!" said Daisy as she came into the Clubhouse one day. "This pumpkin won the grand prize at the County Fair!"
"Hot dog!" said Mickey. "That is one big pumpkin!"

Donald took a look at the picture.

"Aw, phooey!" he said. "I could grow a garden filled with the biggest pumpkins you've ever seen!" Donald declared. "I'm sure it's easy to do."

The next day, Donald got pumpkin seeds and threw them on the dirt.
"I think it takes more than that to grow a garden," said Minnie.
Mickey nodded. "First you need to make holes in the dirt, put a seed in each hole and then cover them up."

"That's a lot of work," said Donald.
"Maybe Toodles can help," said Mickey. "Oh, Toodles!"

Toodles showed them a pogo stick, a mirror and an elephant.

"Hmm," Donald said. "Which Mouseketool can help us make holes for the seeds?"

"I think it's this one," said Minnie, as she pointed to the pogo stick.

Minnie was right! The pogo stick made holes that were just the right size. Then Donald dropped a seed into each hole and covered them all with dirt.

"See, I told you this would be easy," said Donald as he sat back down. "Now all we have to do is watch the seeds grow."

Donald, thinking his work was done, closed his eyes to rest.
"I think it takes more than that to grow a garden," said Daisy.
"A garden needs water," Mickey said. "Water helps seeds grow."

"Mickey's right," said Minnie.
"But how am I going to water this big garden?" asked Donald.
"That's a lot of work."

"It's time to call Toodles again," said Mickey. "Oh, Toodles!"

"Let's pick the elephant," said Daisy, looking at the remaining tools. Daisy was right! First the elephant took a big drink from the pond. Then, using her trunk, she sprinkled water over the entire garden.

"I told you this would be easy," said Donald as he sat back down.
"I think it takes more than that to grow a garden," said Mickey.
Donald looked puzzled. "But what else is there to do?"

"Plants need sun," said Minnie. "But your garden is in the shade."
"But we can't move the sun!" exclaimed Donald.
"Maybe we can," said Mickey. "Oh, Toodles!"

Toodles had just one tool left – a mirror.

"A mirror?" asked Donald. "How can that help my garden grow?"

Mickey and Minnie placed the mirror so that it reflected the sunlight onto the garden.

"Oh, boy!" shouted Donald. "Now we'll just watch the seeds grow."
Daisy giggled. "Now we have to make sure the garden keeps
getting plenty of water and sunlight and care, Farmer Donald!"

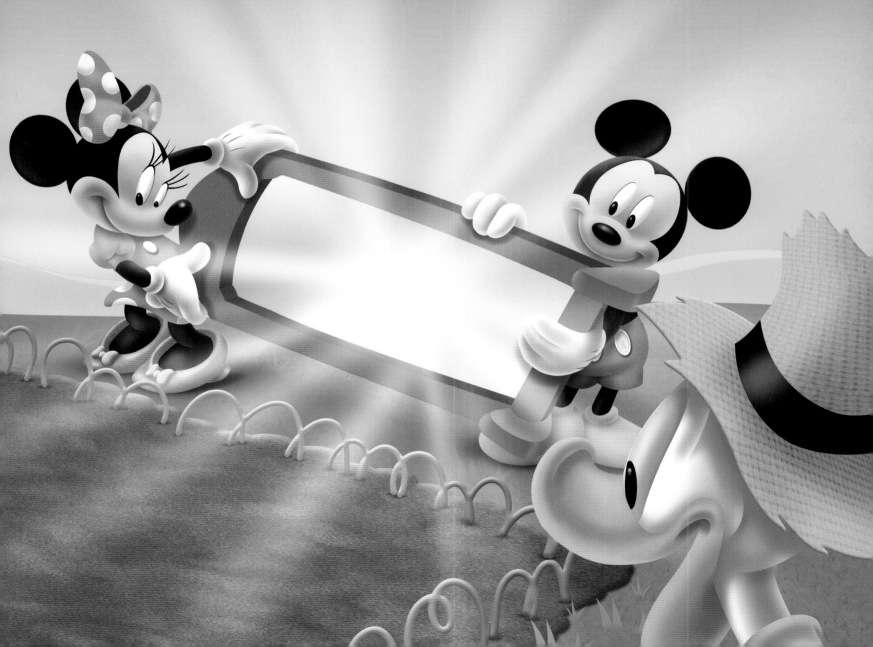

Donald discovered that growing a garden wasn't as easy as he expected. But over the next few months, he worked hard. When it was time for the pumpkin contest, Donald picked the biggest, most beautiful pumpkin from his garden, and then the whole gang headed to the fair.

Judge Goofy walked around and looked at all the pumpkins. Finally he said, "The prize for the biggest pumpkin goes to Farmer Donald!"

"Next year, I think I'll enter the apple-pie contest," said Daisy.

"Good idea!" Donald declared. "I'll plant a great big apple orchard so you'll have all the apples you need. I'm sure it's easy to do."

The End

Look Before You Leap!

By Sheila Sweeny Higginson
Illustrated by the Disney Storybook Artists
Designed by Elizabeth Andaluz

Mickey and Goofy were enjoying a quiet game of chess. Just as Mickey was about to make a move, something soared through the window and landed right in the middle of the chessboard.

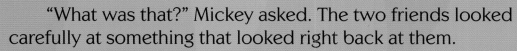

"What was that?" Mickey asked. The two friends looked carefully at something that looked right back at them.

It was green.

It had webbed feet.

It said, "Ribbit, ribbit."

It was a frog – a very jumpy frog. Goofy tried to grab it.

PLOP!

The frog leaped out of Goofy's hands and right onto the silly switch. The room began to spin around. Mickey tried to grab the frog, but it leaped right towards the...

...kitchen sink. *KERPLUNK!*

"You really should look before you leap!" Mickey said to the frog.

"What are we going to do about this big puddle?" Goofy asked.

"Oh, Toodles!" Mickey called. "We need some Mouseketools –
right now!"

"The mop is the right tool for this job," said Mickey. "Thanks, Toodles!"
All of Mickey's hard work made Goofy hungry. He decided
to make lunch. Just then, the frog took a giant leap right towards...

...Goofy's sandwich. *SQUISH!*

"Stop!" Mickey cried as Goofy was about to take a bite.

"You really should look before you leap," Goofy said to the frog, "and I should look before I bite!"

Goofy carried the frog outside.
"Hold on tight," Mickey said. "He's pretty slippery."
"I have him.... I have him.... OOPS! I don't have
him!" Goofy yelped as the frog leaped right towards...

...Daisy's painting! *SPLAT!*

"You should look before you leap!" Daisy said as the paint splattered all around. "Now my painting – and my clothes – are a mess."

"Hey there, little friend," Mickey said to the frog.
"Slow down!"
     But it was too late. The frog leaped out from behind
Daisy's painting and headed straight towards...

...Mickey's bicycle. *BOING!*

He zoomed down the road, holding tightly to the handlebars. He was headed straight for a cliff.

"Oh, no!" Goofy shouted.

"Oh, Toodles!" yelled Mickey. "We need you!"

"The lasso is the right tool for this job," said Mickey. "Thanks, Toodles!"

Mickey and Goofy carefully pulled the bicycle back from the edge of the cliff.

"I think we should help our friend the frog find a nice, safe pond," Mickey said. "Then he can leap without causing any trouble."

The frog jumped up and down in agreement. Then he hopped away down the road with Mickey and Goofy following fast behind him.

The frog stopped hopping right in front of the pizzeria. Slowly, Mickey and Goofy crept up behind him.

"We've got to get him before he leaps!" Mickey whispered.

But it was too late. Just as Mickey reached for him, the frog leaped right onto...

...one of the pizzas. *SLOSH!*

"You should look before you leap!" shouted the man behind the counter as tomato sauce dripped off the pizza. The frog stopped for a moment to lick himself off. Then he hopped down Main Street, headed right toward Minnie and Pluto.

"Maybe Minnie and Pluto can help us catch our frog friend and bring him to a nice pond," Mickey shouted.

But the frog had other ideas. He took a great big leap and landed right inside...

...the goldfish bowl. *SPLASH!*

The big wave made the goldfish fly right out. Minnie gently put the goldfish back into its bowl. "I don't know if we'll ever find a pond for froggie. We need some help!" Goofy sighed.

"Oh, Toodles!" Mickey called.

"The net is the right tool for this job," said Mickey.
At last, they held the frog safely in the net.
   "He seems sad," Goofy said.
   "I think you're right, Goofy," Mickey agreed.
   Then he looked up ahead and saw something that
made him – and the frog – smile.
   "I think we've found just the right place for you,
froggie," Mickey said.

The friends walked quickly down the street towards the fountain. Carefully, Mickey placed the net on the ground and began to lift the frog out. But the frog was impatient. Out he hopped, heading straight for the...

...fountain. He landed with a *SWOOSH!* right next to another frog.

"Ribbit, ribbit," he said.

"Ribbit, ribbit," she replied.

"Maybe we didn't find a pond," said Mickey, "but we did find a good place for him to splash and leap."

"We've found the frog a friend, too," noticed Minnie. "And they look very happy to see each other!"

"I think Minnie's goldfish is happy, too!" added Goofy.

Back at the Clubhouse, Mickey and Goofy got back to their chess game. "C'mon, Mickey," Goofy said, "you haven't made a move in a long time." "I know. I know," replied Mickey. "I just want to make sure I look carefully before I leap!"

The End

Minnie's Rainbow

By Sheila Sweeny Higginson
Illustrated by Loter, Inc.

Minnie has just finished reading a book.
She's asked all her friends to come take a look.

Read About Rainbows

She learned about something you see in the sky,
A colourful arc that the birds fly right by.

But what makes a rainbow that follows the rain?
Let's find out as Minnie and her friends explain.

Red makes a rainbow so fiery bright.
It's for strawberries, stop signs and Mickey's night-light.

Can you find a rainbow near Mickey's bed?
If you do, then you'll see its first colour is red!

A rainbow has orange. It's cheerful and cute –
The colour of tigers and sunsets and fruit.

Now look for the rainbow on Goofy's car.
Then see the colour of its second bar.

Yellow gives rainbows their light, happy rays,
A reminder of ducklings and warm, sunny days.

If you spy the small rainbow that's on Pluto's bow,
You'll find the third colour is one that you know!

There's a garden of green in each rainbow you see.
It's for pickles and peas and the leaves of a tree.

122

So search for the rainbow that's next to the beans,
Then name the fourth colour. That's right, it is green!

Inside every rainbow is cool, calming blue,
For blue skies and bluebells and blue dungarees, too.

124

Now hunt for a rainbow beside Donald's hand.
It's clear now that blue is the rainbow's fifth band.

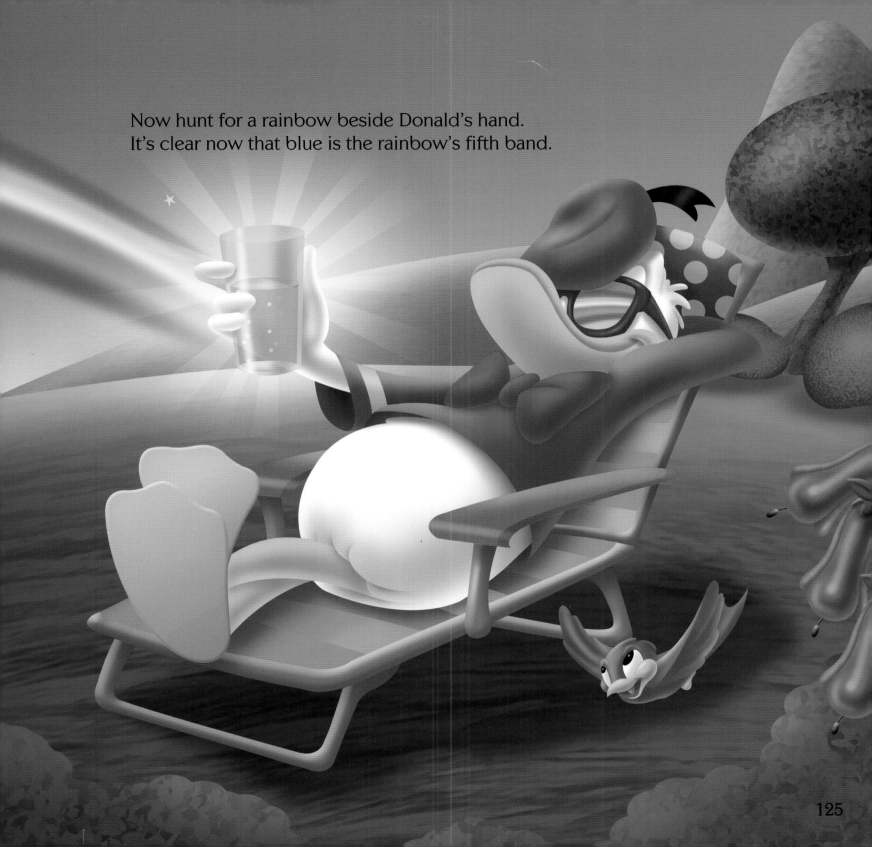

Violet you'll find at the end of the line.
It's the colour of lilacs and grapes on a vine.

126

There's a rainbow hiding under Daisy's beak,
And violet's the sixth of its colourful streaks.

Red, orange and yellow are one, two and three.
Green is four. Blue is five. Violet's six, as you can see.

But there's more to each rainbow you see in the sky.
A whole spectrum of colours, so let's find out why!

A rainbow is made of the colours of light.
When we look at it whole, we can see only white.

But when white light is split, then more colours appear.
If you tried counting them, it might take a whole year!

There are not only colours like red, green and blue.
There are some you can't see with your eyes. Yes, it's true!

So what makes a rainbow? What is it we see?
All the waves that are part of the light, naturally!

The End

Up, Up and Away!

An Adventure in Shadows and Shapes
By Sheila Sweeny Higginson
Illustrated by the Disney Storybook Artists
Designed by Elizabeth Andaluz

Donald and his friends were standing outside the
Clubhouse on a crisp, bright day.
   "Oh, Donald," Daisy said, "look at the sky! It's lovely!"
   "Shhh!" Donald whispered. "Don't make a move! Something
is following me, and I'm going to find out who – or what – it is!"

Daisy giggled as she looked behind Donald.

"Oh, my!" said Daisy. "There is something following you! It's wearing a sailor's cap – just like yours. It's got cute webbed feet – just like yours. And when you move, it moves too."

"Aw, phooey," Donald quacked as he turned around and saw his shadow. "That is a fine-looking shape, but I still don't trust it!"

The friends laughed at Donald as he glared at his shadow.

"Cheer up, buddy," Mickey said. "Why don't you leave your shadow on the ground and come with me?"

"I don't know." Donald moped. "Where are we going?"

"Up, up, and away!" Mickey cheered. "Who wants to help Minnie and me fly our hot-air balloon?"

"I sure do!" shouted Goofy.

"You can count me out," Donald grumbled. "I don't trust that thing. Besides," he added, "I'm not missing lunch."

"Aw, come on, Donald," Minnie pleaded, "I've packed a square meal for each of us. Up, up and away!"

"Something's wrong," Mickey said. "The balloon won't fill with air!"

"That's too bad, buddy," said Donald, trying to hide a grin. "I guess we'll just have to go back to the Clubhouse for lunch."

"Oh, Toodles!" Mickey said. "Do we have a Mousketool that can help?" Toodles appeared.

"Do any of you know how we can use this tool?" Mickey asked.

"I know, Mickey!" answered Minnie. "We can turn the crank to inflate the balloon with hot air."

"Why, you're right, Minnie!" Mickey shouted. "We've got ears! Say cheers!"

Soon, the friends were floating high above the Clubhouse. "Up, up, and away!" cried Daisy. "This is fun!"

"Look, everyone!" yelled Minnie. "Can you see the Clubhouse from here? It looks so small! And there are so many shapes below us. I see a heart, a triangle and a rectangle. What do you see?"

"I see a triangle, too!" Mickey shouted. "And there are Chip and Dale playing a round of golf!"

"It should be called a triangle of golf," laughed Daisy. "Just look at all those triangle-shaped flags!"

"What's a triangle?" asked Goofy, as he bit into his sandwich.

"A triangle is a shape with three sides that all have points at the ends – sort of like your sandwich," Minnie explained.

145

"Or like that?" Goofy questioned, as he pointed to a huge triangle in front of the balloon.

It was the top of a mountain! Suddenly, a gust of wind whisked the friends right towards it!

"We need help," cried Mickey. "Oh, Toodles!"

Toodles appeared with a triangle, a patch, a ladder and a spyglass.

"Which tool should we use?" asked Minnie.

"Let's try them all!" said Mickey. "Daisy, ring the triangle for help!"
Daisy rang the triangle, but it didn't help them get off the mountain.
"Minnie, patch the hole!"
Minnie put a square patch on the round hole in the balloon, but it was too small.
"Goofy, look through the spyglass!" Goofy held the spyglass and saw that the ground looked very far away.
"There's only one tool left," yelled Mickey. "To the ladder!"

Mickey dropped the ladder over the side of the balloon.

"We've got ears! Say cheers!" said Mickey. "If we can't get the balloon to go back up, then we'll have to go down – one step at a time."

"Me first! Me first!" shouted Donald.

"We're going to do this fair and square," Mickey announced. "Take a piece of paper with a number on it. Whoever gets number one goes first. Whoever gets number two goes second. Get the idea?"

The friends headed down the ladder one by one. Everyone was happy to be standing on firm ground again. "We're in great shape, unlike our balloon," said Mickey. "But we're going to have to hike back home. It's not far – just down that path... or maybe it's that other one..."

The friends trudged along, growing more and more tired.
"I think we've been walking in circles," Mickey finally said.
"I'm sure I've seen this tree before."

"Oh, Toodles!"

Toodles appeared, showing three pictures of Mickey. Mickey shared them with his friends.

"I'm standing in front of the Clubhouse and my shadow is different in each picture. In the morning, my shadow falls in front of me. At noon, I have no shadow. In the evening, my shadow falls behind me. Do any of you know what this could mean?"

The friends studied the pictures carefully.

"I've got it!" Donald shouted. "Right now, it's late and the sun is setting behind us. Toodles shows that in the evening, our shadows point towards the Clubhouse. If we follow them, they'll lead us back home."

Donald was correct. The shadows helped the friends head in the right direction. Soon, they arrived back at the Clubhouse. Everyone was hungry from the long trip.

"Well, Donald," Daisy said, "do you trust your shadow now?"

"I'll trust the handsome guy to lead me home," Donald answered. "But he better not ask me to share my pie!"

The End